W9-ADN-452

DISCARD

When Someone Is Afraid

By Valeri Gorbachev
Illustrated by Kostya Gorbachev

Star Bright Books
New York

Text copyright © 2005 Valeri Gorbachev. Art copyright © 2005 Kostya Gorbachev.
All rights reserved. No part of this book may be reproduced or transmitted in any form or by any means, electronic or mechanical, photocopying, recording, or by any information storage and retrieval systems that are available now or in the future, without permission in writing from the copyright holders and the publisher.

Published in the United States of America by Star Bright Books, Inc.,
30-19 48th Avenue, Long Isand City, NY 11101.

The name Star Bright Books and the Star Bright Books logo are registered trademarks of Star Bright Books, Inc.

Please visit www.starbrightbooks.com. For bulk orders, call email: orders@starbrightbooks.com, or call customer service at: (718) 784-9112.

HC ISBN-13: 978-1-932065-99-2
HC ISBN-10: 1-932065-99-7
Star Bright Books / NY / 00208110
Printed in China (WKT) 10 9 8 7 6 5 4 3 2

PB ISBN: 978-1-59572-344-4
Star Bright Books / NY / 00108110
Printed in China (WKT) 10 9 8 7 6 5 4 3 2 1

Library of Congress Cataloging-in-Publication Data

Gorbachev, Valeri.
When someone is afraid / by Valeri & Kostya Gorbachev.
p. cm.
Summary: Suggests some of the ways that animals react to fear, but when a small boy wakes from a bad dream he calls for his mommy and daddy.
ISBN 1-932065-99-7
[1. Fear--Fiction. 2. Fear of the dark--Fiction. 3. Dreams--Fiction.] I. Gorbachev, Kostya, ill. II. Title.

PZ7.G6475Wg 2004
[E]--dc22

2004017158

When an ostrich is afraid. . .

it buries its head in the sand.

When a giraffe is afraid. . .

it runs away as fast as it can.

When fish are afraid. . .

they dart away.

When crows are afraid. . .

they fly away.

When a rabbit is afraid. . .

it races into the bushes.

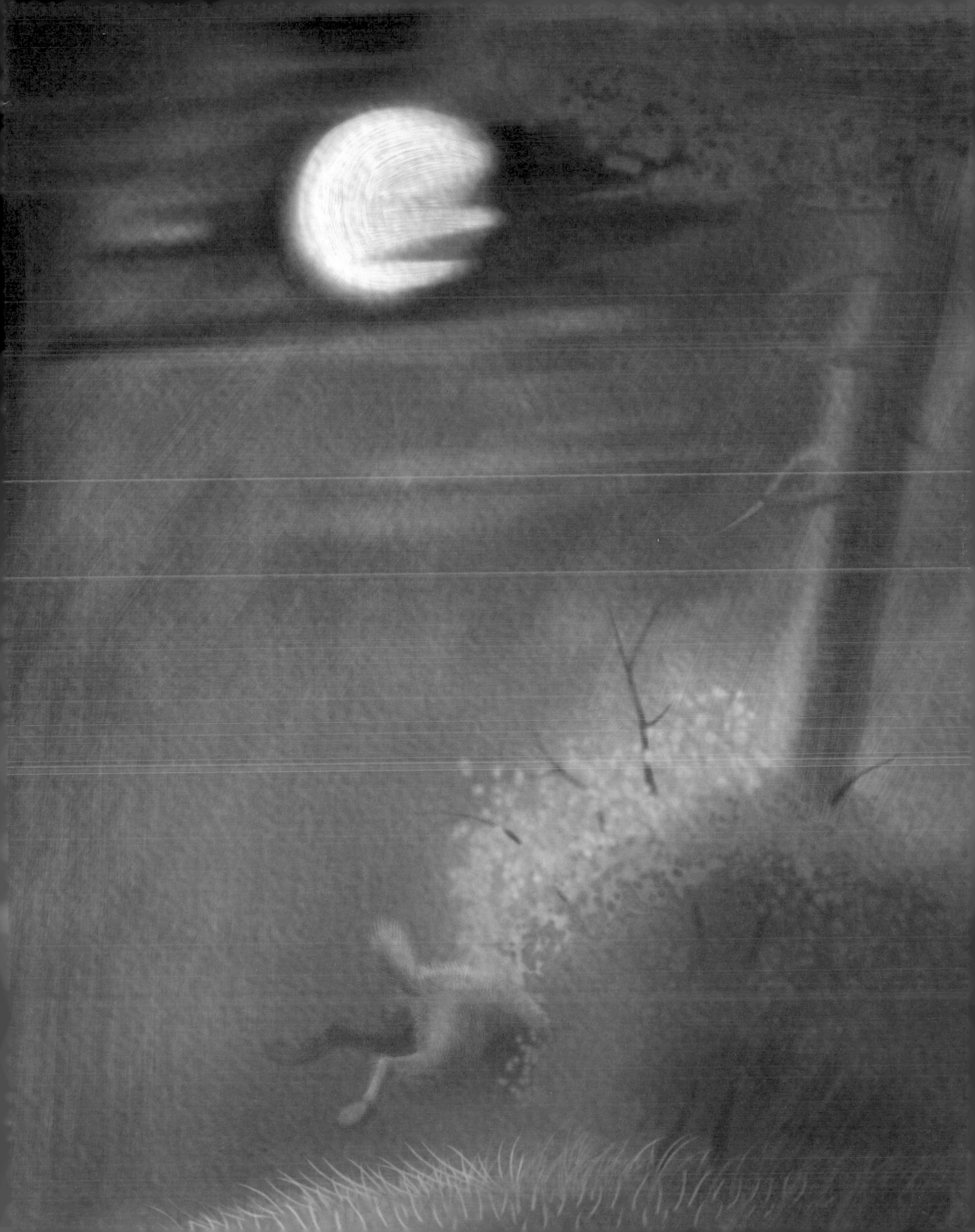

When a turtle is afraid. . .

it shrinks into its shell.

When a squirrel is afraid. . .

it scampers up a tree.

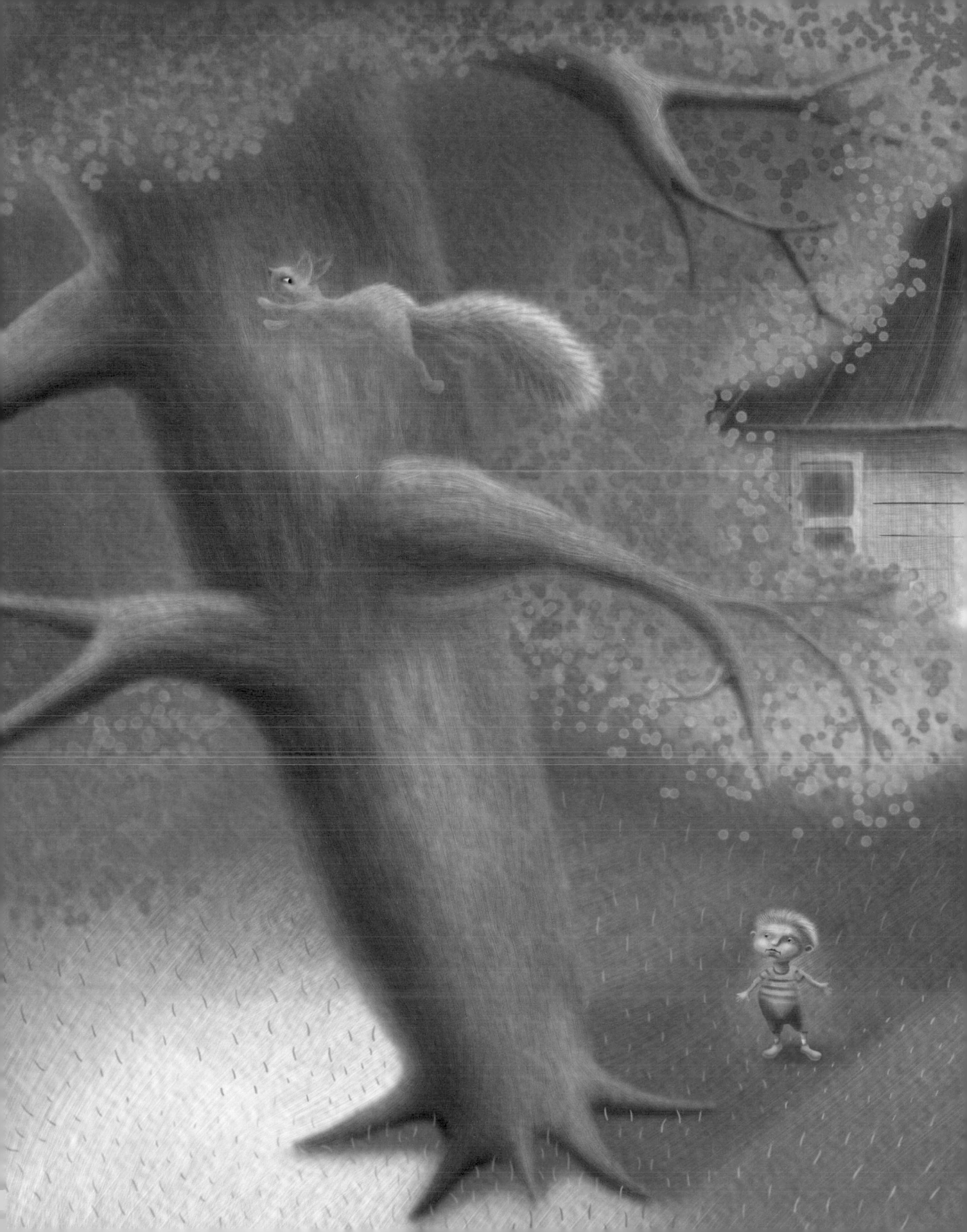

When a mouse is afraid. . .

it hurries into a hole.

When my kitten is afraid. . .

she hides under my bed.

When my dog is afraid. . .

he hides behind me.

When I get scared,
I call Mommy or Daddy.

"MOMMY!"

"What's wrong,
honey?"

"I had a
bad dream."

Mommy gives me a hug. . .

and a kiss. . .

and I am not afraid anymore.

by James Martin
© 1993 by Art Wolfe

part of this book may be
ed in any form or by any
chanical, including
g, or by any information
stem, without permission in
er. Published by Crown
om House company, 201
ork, New York 10022
k of Crown Publishers, Inc.
Kong

aloging-in-Publication Data

e in the Wild / by James
Art Wolfe.

tographs explore how
to survive.
)—Juvenile literature. 2.
enile literature.
y) 2. Animal defenses.]

92-38211

rade)
b. bdg.)

2 1 FIRST EDITION

mantis hiding against
petals. *Right:* Holding
ith its powerful front